Temporary

Slave

The Pure Pleasure

The most beautiful
stories begin with
courage

IMPRINT

Text and Content

@ COPYRIGHT 2024

BY MARIA VALLEETSY

C/O IMPRESSUM-SERVICE VALLEETSY

PADRE BURGOS AVE,

1000 METRO MANILA

Temporary Slave

Because my husband and I work all day and therefore don't have enough time to look after our children all the time, we thought about different things as to how we could best care for our children during the time when we are not at home.

After a lot of back and forth, we decided on an au pair, as this meant that our children would at least be in familiar surroundings and would not be exposed to constantly changing caregivers.

Long preamble, short story: After about two months, the au pair girl from France finally arrived.

I picked her up from the airport and was blown away when I saw her.
You can't imagine what a beauty she was (and of course still is

now). About 1.70m tall with a slim, toned figure, a shapely butt, very nice breasts (I now know that they are a cup size C, I was just guessing at the time), bright light blue eyes (about the size of the sky). the best days) and brownish hair (about the color of good whiskey).

Plus a really nice pout and a straight, well-shaped nose. Every top model can hide behind her because no one is as beautiful as her. Forget Heidi Klum, Cindy Crawford or whatever their names are. Nobody is as beautiful as Sophie.

The name alone...

Please excuse me for raving so much and digressing from my story, but perhaps this will make it a little easier for you to understand. Yes, many of you have probably checked to see if it is really a woman who is writing this or if you have misread it, because how can a heterosexual woman rave about another woman like that? Well, I can tell you that I have since found out that I am bi. So you didn't read it wrong.

Stop, I have to stop myself here so I can tell you the whole story. It's no use if I write everything down here in a jumbled manner and then you lose track and so do I. So where was I? Oh yes, exactly, at the airport.

So our au pair approached me shyly and asked me if I was Mrs. Maier. Of course, I could only confirm this and immediately introduced myself and told her

that she could also call me Ina
(short for Carolina).

Sophie just smiled shyly at me
and introduced herself too.

Maybe I should also mention here
that she spoke German without
any accent.

Then I took one of the suitcases
from her (she only had two with
her) and walked with her to my
car.

On the drive to my house she
wanted to know a few things

about my family. That was only right for me, because somehow it made me uncomfortable that I was aroused just by looking at her. Especially because I hadn't known anything like that before. Through thoughts and stories about my family, I got myself back under control and my excitement subsided very quickly.

Although... I can't say that it had really subsided, but at least that's how I felt at the time. One would hardly think how we humans sometimes lie to ourselves. But you've probably encountered one situation or another where you've lied to yourself. If this isn't the case, then I'm sorry for wrongly accusing you.

In any case, I told her that my husband and I had known each other for twenty years, had been together for fifteen years and had been married for ten years.
I also told her that we have three children in total, a boy who is eight years old and two girls who are five and one year old. Until now, my mother had always looked after the three of them,

but she simply no longer felt able to do so due to her health.

We ourselves cannot look after our children all day because my husband is a doctor and I am an advertising agent and we both love and need our jobs too much.

Our children are the most important thing to us, but without our jobs we would be unhappy and, in our opinion, this would be passed on to our children in one way or another.

She also wanted to know what her tasks would be with us. This question was clarified very quickly, because their tasks include all areas that affect the household and the children, i.e. running some housework (they also have a cleaner who comes twice a week), cooking for the children and us, and homework do, take the children to their leisure activities and and and.

Just everything that happens to a family. You probably know best what needs to happen to you and our au pair also has these tasks.

This cannot be completely avoided simply because, as already mentioned, my husband and I are very busy at work and want to spend the little time we have left with our children or with each other.

Finally we arrived at my home and my husband and children were already waiting for us.

Strangely enough, my husband only briefly looked Sophie up and down, but then he was extremely friendly and accommodating and didn't show any further reaction.

This surprised me a lot since I was sexually attracted to her myself and as a heterosexual woman!!

Another question from you is certainly how I can talk about it so casually and that it was certainly different for me in this situation. You're right, but six months have now passed and I can only smile at my naivety and insecurity at the time. But back again...

After greeting us, we brought Sophie's things into her small apartment (we have a separate apartment in the house) and then we all went into the living room together. There, at her own request, Sophie first worked with the children so that they could get to know her better.

My husband and I retreated to the kitchen and meanwhile prepared dinner. There we talked about our first impressions of Sophie. This time too, I realized that she didn't seem to make any particular impression on my husband from a purely external perspective.

A short time later the food was ready and we all had dinner together. Sophie was already very popular with the children and we all laughed a lot together. Even my son, who is usually skeptical of strangers, was really excited.

Afterwards, my husband and son set the table and Sophie and I went into the bathroom with my girls to get them ready for bed.

I probably have to briefly explain to you that we always have a fixed routine in the evenings. It is very important to my husband and I that we all eat dinner together. Only in extreme emergencies is one of us not there.

After dinner, either my husband or I and our son clean up everything and the other puts the girls to bed. First they go to the bathroom, where they get ready for bed, and then to their room, because at the moment they still have one thing in common. We then play together there for about half an hour. Afterwards they go to bed and they tell a story, sing something and then pray. This ritual is very important to us because it allows us to spend more intensive time together.

After the girls went to sleep, Sophie and I went into the living room where my husband was waiting for us alone. My son already went to his room because he wanted to do something.

So Sophie and I sat down with my husband and asked her to tell us something about herself so

that we could get to know her
better.

She did this hesitantly at first, but
as the story progressed it just
came pouring out of her.

I'm going to put it all together
here for you in a nutshell so that
you don't have too much to read
and I don't have too much to
write. I hope you can understand
this.

At nineteen years old, Sophie is
the oldest of four children and the
only girl. Her father believes that

girls are less valuable than men and has made her and her mother feel this too. She was always oppressed by him, and later also by her brothers. After her relationship with her boyfriend broke down, she signed up for the au pair program and ended up with us.

As I said, I only gave you the short version here. In fact, the conversation lasted several hours that evening and we finally agreed that we would all go to bed.

The next few weeks went relatively smoothly. At first I stayed at home, but when I realized that my children completely trusted Sophie, I went back to work.

This suited me very well because I noticed that Sophie's presence was arousing me more and more and for the first time I felt real desire for a woman. This was particularly bad for me because she was such a young woman, after all, I'm already 40 and could therefore be her mother, and I actually still love my husband very much. So I blamed myself a lot and became more and more insecure when dealing with her because I didn't want her to notice anything.

My work came in handy because it meant I was no longer with her all day. But that didn't help either. On the contrary, I couldn't really concentrate anymore and was always waiting longingly for me to get home again. Even in the office I sometimes had erotic fantasies in which Sophie played the main role. For example, I once imagined her pleasuring me orally.

You may also need to know that I generally take a passive role in sex because I don't like being the active one. It just makes me feel uncomfortable and I can't really enjoy it all.

My husband also noticed the change in me because at some point he asked me directly what was wrong with me. You can imagine my horror when this happened and I just stammered. This certainly didn't convince him, but he dropped the topic for my sake.

By the way, Sophie also played her part in ensuring that I couldn't banish her from my thoughts. I now know that this was ice-cold calculation on her part.

Wondering what she did? Well, I would like to tell you that too.

It started with her wearing shorter and shorter things. At first she was always dressed high-necked, but at some point her pants became shorter and her blouses and T-shirts became more low-cut. However, she mainly only wore things like that when she knew that my husband wasn't around and wouldn't be coming anytime soon. Otherwise, she has become more revealing, but not as much. Actually, I should have been aware of the whole thing back then, but I wasn't. You're always wiser in hindsight. When my husband took our children to his parents' house for a week, things got even worse.

When I came back from the office in the evening, Sophie was always waiting for me to eat. She then wore increasingly transparent tops and no longer wore a bra underneath. Well, she can afford it with her breasts, but can you imagine what happened to me? You're probably thinking that I should have said something, but at that point I didn't want to admit to her, and especially to myself, that she could confuse and unsettle me so much. After all, I am much older and therefore have a lot more life experience. I can only repeat myself: I was incredibly naive back then. Now back to what else she did...

In addition, when we were watching TV together in the evening, she would often sit across from me and spread her legs. Since she wasn't wearing any panties, I could see her shaved vagina very clearly, which only made me even more excited. Of course, I again acted as if nothing was happening, but the calculating beast of course noticed everything very clearly.

When she came into the bathroom naked one morning while I was taking a shower, it was all too late. It was just bubbling inside me and when she left the bathroom shortly afterwards, I couldn't contain myself any longer and masturbated myself.

I started stroking myself gently. At first just over my breasts and then I quickly started playing with my nipples while the water was just pelting over my body.

I imagined that it was Sophie's hands gently touching and pampering me. This thought excited me so incredibly that at some point I slid my hands further down until I finally landed in my pubic area and began to gently stroke myself there. My thoughts were still circling around Sophie and I imagined myself asking her to touch my clit.

I then started gently massaging my clitoris. When I couldn't do that anymore, I started fingering myself. When I was finally close to the liberating orgasm, the door

opened and Sophie was standing
in the doorway.

You can certainly imagine how
frightened I must have looked
and how I immediately took my
hands away. It was just a fantasy
and now Sophie was standing in
front of me in the flesh! I was
completely frozen and quickly
looked for excuses.

But based on the soft moans that
she must have heard when she
came in, I couldn't even say that I
was just soaping myself up. I

couldn't think of any other excuses at that moment.

But when I looked at her I was extremely surprised because she started laughing spitefully and then just said succinctly that she already thought that I was into her, the way I always stared at her.

At that moment I thought I wasn't hearing properly and wanted to throw her out of the bathroom, but she beat me to it. She just walked up to me, took me in her arms and kissed me like it was the most normal thing in the world.

However, she didn't act gently, as I always imagined, but rather she was somehow rough and possessive. I've never experienced a kiss like that before.

At first I resisted it because I was really outraged by her statement and at the same time embarrassed, but my excitement quickly won out and I agreed to the kiss. This became more and more intense and at some point she started caressing me all over my body.

As you all know by now, I am happily married and therefore resisted, but she quickly broke this resistance by simply continuing to kiss and caress me.

It wasn't that difficult for her to break the resistance because, as already mentioned, I had dreamed shortly before that she was touching me gently and pampering me.

I have to confess to you that I even had to think about her during sexual intercourse with my husband. These were not dominant fantasies at the beginning. However, since, as already mentioned, I am more of a passive person when it comes to sex, I let her guide me in my fantasies and pamper me without dominance or humiliation playing a role.

I have to and would like to mention this clearly here again, because I realized to my horror that this was exactly what turned me on even more, which meant that she had already indirectly subjugated me, even if I was still fighting against it internally.

At some point her hand was suddenly in my pubic area and she first gently stroked me there and then moved on to massaging my clitoris. However, at some point she stopped being gentle and actually abused him by pinching him and repeatedly pulling him in an extremely painful way. Nevertheless, it didn't take long until I reached my orgasm with a loud moan.

And do you know what the beast did then? She just laughed and whispered that she had me now and then went to the bathroom.

Can you imagine how I felt? I recently cheated on my husband with a WOMAN who happens to be our au pair and who I had been longing for for a while and she treats me like a piece of trash and humiliates me. Well, I felt like a piece of trash myself, or rather like a slut! But what was even worse: the way she treated me excited me to the utmost again!

The worst part, however, was that these humiliations excited me far more than the tender games of my dreams. This somehow made me feel even more like a traitor and somehow made me doubt my sanity because I, an intelligent, normal woman, couldn't possibly have liked that.

From then on I avoided Sophie as much as possible and was extremely happy that my husband and children came back just a day later. Although I had an extremely bad conscience towards my husband, at the same time I didn't dare say anything to him.

By the way, Sophie has always provoked me sexually in one way or another. From then on she walked around only very lightly dressed - even worse than before and now also when my husband was there - and never missed an opportunity to touch me.

You're probably wondering why I didn't give her notice. But how was I supposed to do that? My husband would not have understood this and would definitely have wanted an explanation.

And my children had taken her incredibly close to their hearts and I would have hurt them very much. Another crucial factor was that I simply didn't want it, which I can only really admit to myself now. At that time, the first two factors were only decisive for me.

Or at least that's what I convinced myself.

I needed the feeling that she was near me and also these little, at least in my eyes, humiliations that she had shown.

Or rather, I often humiliated myself in some way. Be it during sex with my husband, during which I could only think about Sophie and her dominant manner, or in any other situation in which I embarrassed myself to the extreme just so that I wouldn't be near Sophie had to, but at the same time I didn't want anything else.

At some point my husband had to go to a medical conference. Since my son was on vacation at the time and my daughters didn't necessarily have to go to kindergarten or the youngest is still at home anyway, my in-laws decided that they wanted to have the children with them at that time.

You can certainly imagine my horror at this, as it meant that I would be alone with Sophie again for a whole week. And you now know what happened last time.

At the same time, this thought also excited me incredibly, because now I no longer had to hide my feelings all the time and I also had hope that this game might repeat itself again. However, it was exactly this thought that frightened and shocked me again and I swore to myself that I would not respond to any advances from her. Oh how wrong I was...

At the same time, it was difficult for me to prevent my children from going to their grandparents, so I said goodbye to my husband and children on a Sunday because my husband wanted to bring the children to his parents before he left for his congress is.

I was barely back in the house when Sophie came down the stairs naked and grabbed my arm as I tried to quickly disappear. She just said that I shouldn't act like that since she knew me inside and out by now. He laughed extremely maliciously.

I still tried to turn away again, which was probably too stupid for her. She simply pulled me back towards her and gave me a resounding slap in the face. She then harshly demanded that I finally stop the fuss and undress, because she had noticed exactly how I had been staring at her the whole time while I thought I was unobserved. And ultimately I wouldn't be able to defend myself against them, as the situation in the bathroom back then would have shown all too clearly.

At first I was taken aback. How could she even want something like that from me? After all, I am a married woman. Now, to be honest with you, I was also ashamed of my body. He's still in top shape for a forty-year-old, but the whole thing was embarrassing for me because after all, a nineteen-year-old beauty was standing in front of me and demanding this from me.

At the same time, the rough treatment of Sophie also excited me and I followed her command as if under compulsion.

I then felt the blood rush to my head and I turned bright red.

I just felt helpless at that moment and at the same time I couldn't resist because deep down that's exactly what I wanted. I really enjoyed this treatment and, yes, I have to admit it, my juices were gushing out of my privates and my nipples were stiff like never before.

Because they usually have to be pampered for an extra long time before they even stand up. When I stood naked in front of her, she took me in her arms and kissed me very intensely again.

I didn't resist this kiss. On the contrary, I returned this kiss passionately because I was extremely aroused by her behavior towards me and I also enjoyed it very much. To this day I still don't know why that is, but I've also learned that you don't get an answer to everything.

She simply had me in her hands in this, as well as in many subsequent situations.

I followed every single one of her wishes, or rather orders, and I couldn't react any differently. It was like a compulsion, as if I was completely inferior to her and had to do what she commanded. At the same time, I also felt stronger and more confident than ever before. By the way, a feeling that I still had very often to this day. But let's move on now...

When Sophie broke away from me, I groaned in disappointment and wanted to pull her back, but she pulled away from me and just said that they were playing by her rules here and that I should stick to them if I wasn't going to be punished want.

I just nodded sheepishly and she laughed again. How I now hate her laugh....and yet love it too. Somehow I couldn't react in this situation other than just nodding, because although I was shocked that she gave me the choice, I was also hornier than ever before.

I now know that I have a submissive streak and Sophie has

brought it out. Maybe that's why I reacted one way and not another. I can't describe it to you in detail and I hope you can forgive me.

Shortly afterwards she took my hand and pulled her into the apartment. Oh, I don't think I've mentioned before that you can reach the granny flat from us without any long detours. You can lock it on both sides, but we decided not to do that because Sophie is supposed to be there for the children and now also for me.

When we finally arrived at her apartment, she took me into the bedroom and I stood there, frozen. She had completely repurposed it and there was nothing left in the usual places. In addition, new things were added that made an extremely strange impression on me.

Now I know all too well what these things are for.

In any case, there was a cross in her bedroom - now I know it's a St. Andrew's cross - and various hooks in the ceiling. There was also a new cupboard that had different dildos, vibrators and the like.

Since the drawers were transparent, I was also able to see that there were, among other things, whips and other percussion instruments in them.

You're probably wondering how Sophie was able to get all of this, because when she arrived she only had two suitcases with her and you don't earn that much as an au pair. I would like to tell you that.

My family and I once went away together for a weekend and Sophie stayed home because it really was supposed to be a family weekend and she deserved some free time. And yes, I admit it, I just wanted some distance from her.

During this time her equipment, as she called it, probably arrived, because from the beginning she wanted to submit to me, as I apparently reminded her of her mother in a certain way and she was thus able to indirectly take revenge on her.

Nowadays we don't play the games out of revenge, but because we both enjoy them in one way or another, but that's how it was back then.

She got the equipment from her ex-boyfriend, because he was into games like that, except that she was the slave back then. That was also the reason for the separation, as it simply didn't suit her nature. He then graciously left everything to her because he emigrated to America after the separation. At least that's what she told me afterwards. I can't tell you exactly whether it's true. Now back to what happened that day.

Sophie looked at me with extreme amusement when she noticed my stare and my rigidity and just said that I would have enough fun here in the near future and that I should finally get moving.

When I didn't react straight away, she gave me a push and I

fell towards the table, which, by the way, had just been brought into the bedroom by her because it wasn't there before.

Shortly before the table I found my balance again. However, Sophie didn't let this last long, turned me around and pushed me firmly down onto the table so that I was lying on him with my entire upper body.

Due to the hard but cold surface of the table, a shiver ran through my body.

Then she bent down and put my feet in cuffs that were attached to the table. I tried to defend myself, but I have to honestly admit that it was more of a formality, as I really enjoyed it all and didn't give any thought to any possible consequences for myself at that moment.

While she was fastening my feet to the table legs, I sat up again because I wanted to know what she was doing with me. When she was finally finished, she pushed me back onto the table and took my hands and attached them to the table legs as well.

At that moment I really became aware of my bizarre situation and I really fought against the shackles, but it was too late.

Sophie once again just laughed, looked me up and down and said that they could finally look at me in peace and that I couldn't do anything about it.

This is exactly what she did extensively. Slowly her gaze roamed over my entire body, starting from my face, over my neck and then my upper body, all the way to my privates, where her gaze then lingered.

The whole thing was extremely uncomfortable for me and I just turned back and forth in my bonds, but it didn't help. I was just too fixated.

You wonder why I was uncomfortable with all of this. Well, imagine yourself in a situation like this: completely exposed and spread wide, tied to a table and unable to defend yourself. You will be looked at from top to bottom by a beauty twenty years younger than you and you will have no way of concealing your little weaknesses.

Do you now know why the whole thing made me uncomfortable and how I felt at that moment?!

Suddenly, without a word or any apparent reason, she turned around and ran into the bathroom and messed around there. At that moment I asked myself what she was doing there, but a short time later my question was answered because she came back with a washing bowl and shaving kit.

I probably have to briefly mention here that I wasn't completely shaved at the time, but still had a small strip left, because that made me feel a little more confident and not quite so naked.

Many of you probably don't understand how a single stripe can make you feel safer and less naked, but it was the same for me. Now it's the other way around and I only feel really good when I'm completely bald.

However, Sophie didn't like the strip and she came to me and said that from now on I would always have to be completely shaven and that she would only do it for me this once. If I didn't shave in the future, she would pluck my hair out one by one with tweezers.

I suddenly became so insecure that I began to fidget, which is why Sophie first slapped my privates and said that I should just lie still if I didn't want to get hurt.

This fact immediately made me stop moving because I was incredibly afraid that she would somehow hurt me or even punish me. She then started shaving me.

She was extremely careful and first gently massaged me with the foam and then very carefully shaved off the hair.

To be honest, I can't tell you how I felt at the time because the

whole situation was a
rollercoaster of emotions.

All I remember is that I was
terribly embarrassed that she
shaved me in such an intimate
place and I couldn't even defend
myself against it.
I felt incredibly defenseless,
especially because my last
protection, the little strip that I
had always needed for my safety,
had now been stolen from me. I
know this must sound terribly
dramatic to all of you, but that's
exactly what happened to me in
this situation.

Afterwards she dried her hands and stroked me gently, thinking that this was the only way she could check whether she had actually caught all the hair.

I really enjoyed this touch and somehow it rewarded me for all the previous events. I quickly forgot exactly these events and just concentrated on the touch.

Slowly but surely her finger slid further and further down until it was on my clit and started massaging it gently.

By now I was writhing in my bonds again. This time, however, it was because of excitement because I was incredibly horny and wanted to achieve my release.

But shortly before the time had come, Sophie stopped again and I groaned in horror, which only earned me another slap on my privates.

She then asked me in no uncertain terms to finally understand that we were only playing according to her rules and immediately told me that there would be consequences if I didn't do so.

Then she went to the closet, got a vibrator, put it on a low level and inserted it into me. As a result, I always remained very aroused and on the verge of orgasm, but release did not follow. Afterwards she put away the shaving kit and took a long shower.

It seemed like an eternity before she finally came back. You have to imagine that I was lying on the table extremely horny and just couldn't reach my orgasm.

Nevertheless, or precisely because of that, I had forgotten everything around me and my senses were only focused on Sophie and my body

When she finally came back, I was just a heap of misery who wanted to finally find salvation and would have done anything for it. Sophie knew this all too well because she came to me and sat on my face and told me to lick her until she reached orgasm. If I didn't do it right or if it took too long, I wouldn't be able to experience one even today.

So I got to work straight away because it was clear to me that I wouldn't survive the day without an orgasm.

I know you're thinking that this is completely exaggerated and I now realize that too.

But are you in a situation where you are always kept on the verge of orgasm for hours and cannot get or obtain any release. Afterwards you will know how I felt in this current situation and you would react exactly the same as me.

At first I was very hesitant because I had never licked a woman before, but at some point I pampered her the way I always wanted my husband to when he licked me - which, by the way, was rare enough.

First I ran my tongue through her entire crack and tasted a woman's juice for the first time, which was really pleasant, because Sophie was also very excited by the whole situation.

Then I gently nibbled on her clitoris with my teeth and massaged it again and again with my tongue.

It didn't take long for Sophie to shift restlessly with her abdomen on my face and produce more and more juices. Shortly afterwards she came with a loud scream and collapsed on my body, exhausted.

However, she quickly pulled herself together again and got off me. She then looked at me and said that, contrary to expectations, I had done a good job and that I would now be given an orgasm as a gift.

She immediately kept this promise. She went around the table and turned the vibrator to the highest setting and then fucked me with it.

At the same time, she massaged my clit with her other hand and pinched it every now and then.

This interplay of pain and pleasure quickly brought me to an orgasm that I had never experienced so intensely before. Well, I've been on the verge of it the whole time.

After a few moments I got my long-awaited release. At first my whole body contracted and then it reared up. My whole body was covered in a light film of sweat.

It's hard to understand what happened at that moment if you

haven't experienced something
like it before.
It was like a smoldering fire that
suddenly exploded from my
shame throughout my entire
body and this explosion lasted for
a few minutes.

As I said, you can only
understand this if you have
experienced it yourself. Those of
you who haven't had this good
fortune will now think that I'm
exaggerating wildly.

But that's really how it was. Afterwards, I was exhausted and trembled all over and then collapsed.

She then freed me from the table and we went to her bed together, where we fell asleep cuddled up together.

Since that day I have been Sophie's slave, so for four months now.

82